Honey Trouble

Honey Trouble

Dianne Young

Cover art by Kristine Makauskas
Illustrations by Linda K. Aleksa

ROUSSAN
PUBLISHERS INC.
Specializing in YA and fiction for pre-teens

THE CANADA COUNCIL | LE CONSEIL DES ARTS
FOR THE ARTS | DU CANADA
SINCE 1957 | DEPUIS 1957

We acknowledge the support of the Canada Council for the Arts
for our publishing program.

We acknowledge the financial support of the Government of Canada
through the Book Publishing Industry Development Program
for publishing activities.

Roussan Publishers Inc.,
5764 Monkland Ave, Suite 103, Montreal QC H4A 1E9, Canada

http://www.roussan.com

National Library of Canada
Bibliothèque nationale du Québec

Canadian Cataloguing in Publication Data

Young, Dianne, 1959-
Honey trouble
For ages 6-9.

ISBN 1-896184-01-4
I. Title.

PS8597.O5923H66 2001   jC813'.54   C2001-901329-9
PZ7.Y696Ho 2001

Cover design by Dan Clark
Interior design by Jean Shepherd

Published simultaneously in Canada and the United States of America
Printed in Canada

1 2 3 4 5 6 7 8 9 UTP 9 8 7 6 5 4 3 2 1

To Mawsy
with love

1
Josie

"Josie! Josie! Come here please," called Mom. "I'm in the kitchen."

Josie was reading in her bedroom. She put down her comic book and went to the kitchen.

"Josie, we've run out of honey, and I don't have time to go shopping today. Will you go to Bonner's for me, please?"

"Okay," replied Josie. She liked walking to Bonner's Corner Store. It was only two blocks away, and Mrs. Bonner always told her funny jokes.

"Will you remember what to buy? Should I write it down for you?" asked Mom.

"No, I'll remember. You want me to buy honey."

"What if you get to the store and forget what to buy?"

Josie thought for a moment. "I'll think of a bear. Bears love honey. That's how I'll remember to buy honey."

"That's a very good idea," said Mom. "I think you *will* remember what to buy."

Mom took four dollars out of her purse. She gave the money to Josie.

"Remember to look both ways before you cross the street," reminded Mom.

Josie put the money in her pocket. "I will," she said, "and I will remember what to buy."

Josie put on her shoes and went out the front door. As she skipped down the sidewalk she said to herself, "Bear, bear, bear ... bear, bear, bear ... remember ... remember ... bear, bear, bear!"

Danny and Rex

Josie skipped past her neighbor's house. She saw her friend Danny and his dog in the front yard.

"Hi, Danny," said Josie. "What are you doing?"

"Oh hi, Josie. I'm trying to teach Rex a new trick."

"I didn't know he could do tricks." Josie

petted Rex on the head.

"Well, he can't yet," said Danny, "but he's pretty smart. I'm trying to teach him to roll over. Want to see?"

"Sure!" cried Josie. She sat down on the sidewalk to watch.

Danny rolled over on the grass in front of Rex. "See, Rex? Roll over like this." Danny rolled over again. Rex did not move.

"Come on, Rex," said Danny. "You can do it. Roll over like this." Danny rolled over one more time. Rex still did not move.

Josie giggled. "It looks like Rex has taught *you* a new trick!"

"Ha ha. Very funny," replied Danny, sitting up. "Maybe if we both show him, he'll get it."

"Okay," agreed Josie. "Here, Rex. Watch this!" Josie crawled over onto the grass and rolled over in front of Rex.

"Come on, Rex!" cried Danny as he rolled over and over.

"Here, boy!" called Josie as she rolled over

and over and over.

Rex watched Danny and Josie. He tilted his head one way, then the other. Suddenly he began to bark. "Ruff! Ruff!"

"Hurray!" shouted Danny. He stopped rolling and gave Rex a big hug. "We did it, Josie! We did it!"

Josie stopped rolling and looked at Danny.

"What do you mean?" she asked. "Rex didn't roll over."

"That's okay," replied Danny. "We taught him a different trick. We taught him to speak!"

Rex barked again. "Ruff! Ruff!"

"See?" said Danny happily. "I told you he was smart! Good boy, Rex! Good boy!" Danny hugged Rex again.

Josie gave Rex a big hug, too. "That was fun."

"Do you want to play some more?" asked Danny. "We could play on the swings if you want."

"Not right now," said Josie. "I'm going to Bonner's for my mom."

"You're lucky!" exclaimed Danny. "I like going there. Mrs. Bonner tells good jokes. What do you have to get?"

"I have to get ..." started Josie, but then she stopped. "Oh no!" she cried. "I forgot what my mom wants me to buy!"

Bear...Bear...Bear...

"You'd better go home and ask your mom again," said Danny.

"No," said Josie. "I told her I would remember. I will remember. I just have to think."

Josie closed her eyes tight. She thought and thought.

"Bear!" she said suddenly, opening her

eyes. "That's it!"

"You're supposed to buy a bear?" asked Danny loudly.

"No, silly. It was supposed to help me remember what to buy. I just have to think now. Let's see ... bear ... bear ... bear ..."

"Berries!" shouted Danny. "Bear sounds like berries. I bet you were going to Bonner's to buy berries!"

"Maybe ..." said Josie slowly. "My mom does love strawberries."

"I bet that's it then!" exclaimed Danny. "I bet you were going to Bonner's to buy strawberries for your mom!"

"I guess you're right, Danny. Yes, that must be it!"

"Hurray!" shouted Danny. "Say *hurray*, Rex!" Danny rolled over on the grass.

"Ruff! Ruff!" barked Rex.

Josie laughed. "Thanks, Danny."

Danny stood up and bowed. "You're welcome. Do you think you will remember what to buy now?"

"I think so, but I'm going to think of a better way to remember strawberries, just in case."

"Good idea," agreed Danny.

"I know!" exclaimed Josie. "Strawberries are red. If I forget what to buy again, I will think of the color red."

"Good one!" Danny nodded his head. "Now you'll remember what to buy for sure."

"Yes, I will. I'm going to buy strawberries for my mom. See you later, Danny!"

"Bye, Josie!"

"Red, red, red ... red, red, red ... remember ... remember ... red, red, red!" Josie said to herself as she skipped down the sidewalk. "Red, red, red ... red, red, red ... remember ... remember ... red, red, red!"

Mrs. Lee

Josie skipped by the last house on the block. In the front yard was her babysitter, Mrs. Lee. She was down on her hands and knees looking under a lawn chair.

"Hi, Mrs. Lee," said Josie. "What are you looking for?"

Mrs. Lee looked up and smiled. "Hello there, Josie. I've lost my glasses. Maybe you could help me find them. I can't see very well without them."

"Sure, I'll help." Josie opened the little front gate and went into the yard. "How did you lose them?"

"I was sitting here reading," Mrs. Lee explained. "The sun is so nice and warm this morning. I decided to have a little nap. When I woke up, my hat had fallen off and my glasses were gone!"

Josie crawled carefully around the lawn chair, looking for the glasses. "Where did you find your hat?" she asked.

"It was here, beside my chair. I thought maybe my glasses would be here, too." Mrs. Lee sat up and slowly shook her head. "I don't understand where they could have disappeared to!"

Josie looked up at her. She noticed something shiny just above Mrs. Lee's ear.

Josie stood up and grinned. "I think I found your glasses," she said.

"You did? Already? That's wonderful!

Where did you find them?"

Josie reached over and took off Mrs. Lee's hat. There, on top of her head, were her glasses.

"There they are," said Josie, "on your head!"

Mrs. Lee felt the glasses on top of her head. "Oh my, so they are. I must have put them up there before I fell asleep." She laughed and pulled the glasses down onto her nose. "That's better! What a smart girl you are, Josie. Thank you so much for your help. Would you like to come in for a snack?"

"I can't right now," said Josie. "I'm going to Bonner's for my mom."

"Oh, I see. What do you have to get at the store?" asked Mrs. Lee.

"I have to get ..." started Josie, but then she stopped. "Oh no!" she cried, "I forgot what to buy, again!"

Red...Red...Red...

"Maybe you should go home and ask your mother to write a note for you," suggested Mrs. Lee.

"But I told her I would remember!" Josie frowned.

"Well then, you will," said Mrs. Lee. "You're a smart girl, Josie. Just take your time and think now."

Josie closed her eyes to think.

"I remember it had something to do with *red*," she said at last, opening her eyes.

"Could it be *bread*?" asked Mrs. Lee. "Red sounds like bread. Were you going to the store to buy bread?"

"Maybe ..." Josie said slowly. "My mom really likes that special bread that Mrs. Bonner sells."

"Oh, yes. The flax bread," said Mrs. Lee. "It's my favorite, too."

"I guess that must be it then," Josie decided. "I was going to Bonner's to buy flax bread for my mom. Thanks for helping me to remember, Mrs. Lee."

"Oh, you're quite welcome. I'm glad I could help. Would you like me to write it down for you?"

"No, thank you, Mrs. Lee. I want to remember it on my own." Josie paused. "I know! You need bread to make a sandwich. I'll think of a sandwich if I forget again. That will help me to remember to buy bread."

"That's a good way to remember, Josie. Like I said before, you're a smart girl." Mrs. Lee patted Josie on the back.

Josie gave her a hug. "Thanks, Mrs. Lee. I better go now."

"Goodbye, dear," said Mrs. Lee as Josie skipped out the front gate. "Remember to look both ways before you cross the street!"

Josie closed the gate and waved. "I will," she called, "and I'll remember to buy bread.

"Sandwich, sandwich ... sandwich, sandwich ... remember sandwich, sandwich!" said Josie as she skipped along. "Sandwich, sandwich ... sandwich, sandwich ... remember sandwich, sandwich!"

Mr. Rapchuk

Josie stopped at the corner. She looked to the left. No cars were coming. She looked to the right. No cars were coming. Josie quickly crossed the street.

She saw her teacher, Mr. Rapchuk, sitting at the bus stop on the corner. He was reading a book.

"Hi, Mr. Rapchuk," said Josie. "Where are

you going?"

"Hello, Josie," he replied. "I'm just on my way home. I was at the library." He held up his book bag to show Josie.

"What kind of books did you get?" she asked.

"I got three books of legends. They're my favorite kind of story. I just finished reading one about why bald eagles are bald. Would you like to hear it?"

"Sure!" Josie sat down on the bench beside her teacher.

"There once was a wandering magician named Nanabush," began Mr. Rapchuk. "One day Nanabush wandered a little too far and got lost. Just then a big eagle flew by, so Nanabush called out to him. He wanted to ask the eagle for directions, but the eagle pretended not to hear him and kept on flying. That made Nanabush angry, so he changed into a very big eagle and flew after him. The stuck-up eagle saw Nanabush coming and he got scared. He tried to get away by flying way up high in the sky, but Nanabush kept chasing him. Higher and higher he flew. He flew so high that the hot summer sun burned off all the feathers on the top of his head. And that's how bald eagles became bald."

Josie laughed. "That's a good story."

"Would you like to hear another one?" asked Mr. Rapchuk.

"Not right now," said Josie. She hopped off the bench. "I'm going to Bonner's for my mom."

"Oh," said Mr. Rapchuk. "What do you have to get?"

"I have to get …" started Josie, and then she stopped. "Oh no! I forgot again!"

Sandwich...Sandwich...

"Would you like to use my cell phone to call your mom?" asked Mr. Rapchuk.

"No," said Josie. "I told her I would remember. I will remember. I just need to think."

Josie closed her eyes tight.

"It's almost lunch time," said Mr. Rapchuk. "Was it something to eat?"

Josie's eyes popped open. "Sandwich!" she cried.

Mr. Rapchuk shook his head. "I don't think they sell sandwiches at Bonner's, Josie."

"No," she explained, "*sandwich* was supposed to help me remember what to buy."

"Oh, I see. My favorite sandwiches are tuna fish. Were you going to the store to buy tuna?"

"Oh yuk!" Josie wrinkled up her nose. "I hate tuna fish! My favorite sandwiches are baloney."

"Then maybe you were going to the store to buy baloney."

"Maybe ..." said Josie slowly. "My mom usually makes me a baloney sandwich for lunch on Saturday."

"That's today!" exclaimed Mr. Rapchuk.

"That must be it then," Josie decided. "I was going to Bonner's to buy baloney for lunch. Thanks, Mr. Rapchuk."

"No problem, Josie. Will you be able to

remember it now?"

"I think so. But just in case, I'm going to think of a better way to remember baloney." Josie thought for a minute. "I know! Baloney starts with *b*. If I forget what to buy, I'll think of the letter *b*. *B* is for baloney. That's how I'll remember what to buy."

"Good thinking, Josie."

"I'd better go now. Bye, Mr. Rapchuk." Josie waved and skipped away.

"Bye, Josie. See you Monday!"

As she skipped down the sidewalk, Josie said to herself, *"B, b, b ... b, b, b ...* remember ... remember ... *b, b, b!"*

 Mrs. Bonner

Josie pushed open the big glass door of Bonner's Corner Store. *Ting-a-ting!* went the bells on the door.

"Hi there, Josie," said Mrs. Bonner. She was up on a tall ladder in the middle of the store. "What do ghosts like to eat for breakfast?"

Josie walked over to the ladder. She

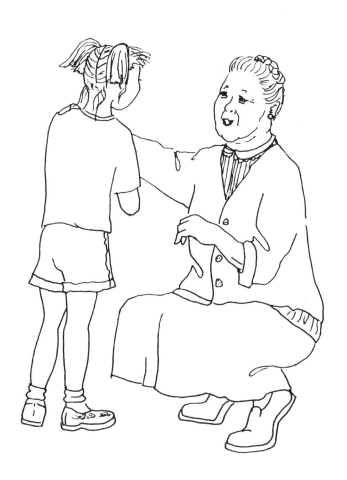

looked up at Mrs. Bonner and smiled. "I don't know."

"Boo-berry pancakes!" Josie and Mrs. Bonner both laughed. "My nephew told me that one."

"It's a good one. What are you doing up there? Changing a light bulb?"

"No. I'm putting up a new sign."

"What does it say?" asked Josie.

"It says GOAT'S MILK NOW FOR SALE."

"Goat's milk? I thought milk came from cows!"

"It does," explained Mrs. Bonner, "but goats also make milk."

"Oh," said Josie. "Maybe my mom will buy goat's milk sometime."

"Where is your mom today, Josie?"

"At home. She's really busy."

"Does she know you're here?"

"Yes," said Josie. "She sent me here."

"Well then, let me get down from this ladder and I'll help you get what you need." Mrs. Bonner climbed down the ladder. She walked over to Josie and squatted down in front of her. "So, what can I get for you to-day?" she asked.

"I came to get ..." started Josie and then she stopped. "Oh no! Not again!"

B... B... B...

"Did you forget what you were supposed to buy?" asked Mrs. Bonner. Josie nodded her head sadly. "That's okay, dear. We can give your mom a call, if you like."

"No," said Josie. "I know I can remember. I forgot before and I remembered. I just have to think."

Once again, Josie closed her eyes tight to

think. "I remember it had something to do with *B,*" she said at last, opening her eyes.

"Bee?" asked Mrs. Bonner. "A bee makes honey. Did you come to get honey?"

"Yes! That's it!" Josie said excitedly. "I remember now. I'm supposed to buy honey! Thanks, Mrs. Bonner."

"Just call me Mrs. Bee!" said Mrs. Bonner, then she buzzed down the next aisle and got a jar of honey off the shelf.

"Buzzzzz! Buzzzzz! Buzzzzz! Come along, Josie Bee!"

Josie laughed and followed her to the counter. "Buzzzzz! Buzzzzz!" She reached in her pocket, pulled out the four dollars and put them on the counter.

Mrs. Bonner entered $3.20 on her cash register. She put Josie's money in the drawer and then counted out eighty cents change. "Twenty-five, fifty, seventy-five and a nickel makes eighty!" Josie put the change in her pocket.

Mrs. Bonner put the honey in a small

paper bag and handed it to Josie. "Here you go, Josie. One jar of honey. That reminds me of another joke. How does a queen bee fix her hair?"

"I don't know." Josie smiled.

"With a honeycomb!" They both laughed again. "Bye now, Josie Bee. Make sure you look both ways before crossing the street, okay?"

"I will," replied Josie. "Bye-bye, Mrs. Bee!" She laughed and buzzed out the door, with the paper bag in her hand. "Buzzzzz! Buzzzzz! Buzzzzz!"

Ting-a-ting! went the bells.

One Jar of Honey 10

Mr. Rapchuk was just getting on the bus when Josie came skipping by.

"Hi, Mr. Rapchuk!"

"Hi, Josie! Did you remember what to buy at the store?"

"Yes!" She held up the paper bag. "One jar full, right here," she said as she skipped away.

"A jar full of baloney?" said Mr. Rapchuk to himself. He shrugged his shoulders and found a seat on the bus.

When Josie got to the corner, she looked to the left. No cars were coming. She looked to the right. One car was coming, so Josie waited for it to go by and then she crossed the street.

Mrs. Lee was sitting on her lawn chair, reading her book when Josie came skipping by.

"Hi, Mrs. Lee."

"Hello, Josie. Did you remember what to buy at the store?"

"Yes!" She held up the paper bag. "One jar full, right here," she said as she skipped away.

"A jar full of bread?" said Mrs. Lee to herself. She shrugged her shoulders and went back to her reading.

Danny was rolling over in front of Rex when Josie came skipping by.

"Hi, Danny."

"Hi, Josie. Did you remember what to buy at the store?"

"Yes!" She held up the paper bag. "One jar full, right here," she said as she skipped away.

"A jar full of strawberries?" said Danny to himself. He shrugged his shoulders and petted Rex's back. "Do you want to play now?" Danny called to Josie.

"Sure! I'll be right back." Josie ran inside her house. "I'm home!" she called.

"Hi, sweetie," said her mom. "Did you remember what to buy at the store?"

"Yes!" said Josie. She handed the bag to her mom. "One jar full of honey, right here."

"Good job, Josie," said her mom. "Did you have any trouble?"

"No," said Josie. She smiled. "No trouble at all."

Dianne Young is a multi-talented lady. After spending sixteen years as a research technician, she returned to school to become a teacher assistant. Now, with her classroom experience at an elementary school in Saskatoon, this lifetime Saskatchewan resident has no shortage of inspiration for her lively, humorous children's stories.

Dianne has published three picture books since she started writing in 1986: *The Abaleda Voluntary Firehouse Band, Purple Hair? I Don't Care!* and *A World of Difference. Honey Trouble,* her fourth book, is her first geared toward early readers.

Visit her website at www3.sk.sympatico.ca/billyou